BLOW THE HAIR DOWN

P9-DJV-402

TASTY TOOTHPASTY 10% REAL JUICE

Wipe AWAY contains no real fruit juice

Miss Malarkey Doesn't Live in Room 10

Miss Malarkey
Doesn't Live in
Room 10

Judy Finchler

Illustrations by Kevin O'Malley

Walker and Company
New York

Artist

by
Pat V.

To my parents, Harriet
and Sid Gold, for her
inspiration as a teacher
and his as a writer.
And of course to
Jerry, Todd, and Lauren.
—J. F.

Text copyright © 1995 by Judy Finchler
Illustrations copyright © 1995 by Kevin O'Malley

First published in the United States of America in 1995 by
Walker Publishing Company, Inc.

Published simultaneously in Canada by Thomas Allen & Son
Canada, Limited, Markham, Ontario

Library of Congress Cataloging-in-Publication Data
Finchler, Judy.
Miss Malarkey doesn't live in room 10 / Judy Finchler ;
illustrations by Kevin O'Malley . p.   cm.
Summary: A first-grade boy is shocked, then pleased, when he
discovers that his teacher has a life away from school.
ISBN 0-8027-8386-4 (hardcover).
— ISBN 0-8027-8387-2 (reinforced)
[1. Teachers—Fiction. 2. Schools—Fiction. 3. Apartment build-
ings—Fiction. 4. Teacher-student relationships—Fiction.]
I. O'Malley, Kevin, 1961- ill. II. Title.
PZ7.F495666Mi 1995
[E]—dc20
94-48703
CIP
AC

Printed in Hong Kong
2 4 6 8 10 9 7 5 3 1

Making a book!

Step 1
write a story

Steep 2
make pictures

maddy

CLASS PROJECTS

Making a Book — Dan V.

agent & arist — drawrings — ediatoor

Book

First u gat a store. Thn u rite Thn u mak pechers

How you m a pictu by shawr

Get so paper

This is a Book

Draw

R Write

This book is for

① Connor
② Noah

-K.O.

I know that Miss Malarkey, my teacher, lives right here at school in Room 10.

That's where she marks our papers
and puts up all the next day's work.

She eats dinner in the cafeteria, and
her table is always the best.

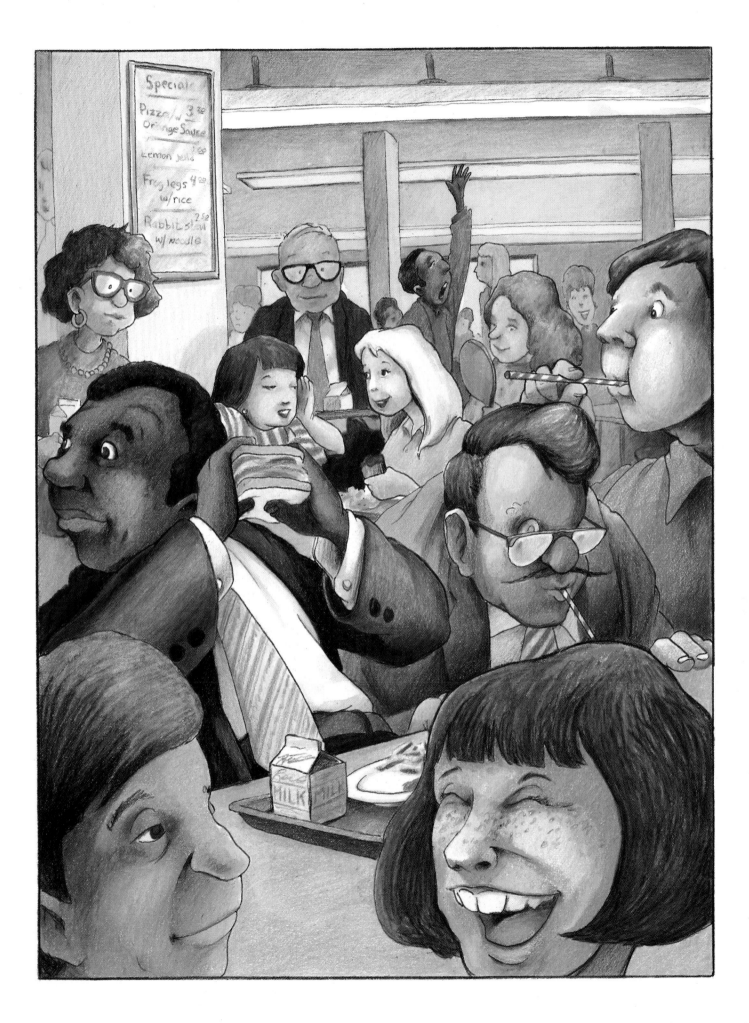

After dinner she plays in the gym with the other teachers. And she never forgets her gym clothes.

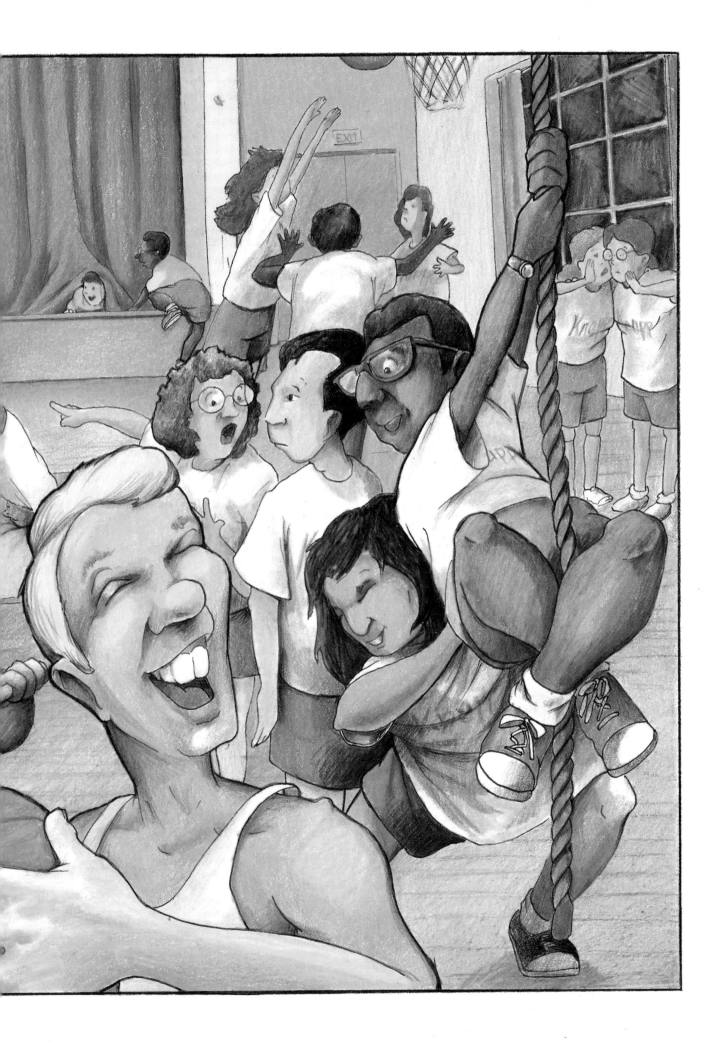

I wonder what the Teachers' Room looks like. That must be where they all sleep. No wonder kids aren't allowed in there. I'm sure teachers don't want us to see their messy room.

Room 10 is a great place to live. It's near the best water fountain in the whole school—the only one that squirts up lots of water.

And the Boys' Room is right across
the hall. . . . Oops!—I mean the Girls'
Room isn't too far away, either.

But last week Miss Malarkey came to our apartment house with a mountain of boxes.

Mom says she's going to live *here* now!

A few days ago when Mom and I baked cookies, she asked me to bring some upstairs to Miss Malarkey. I told her I needed a pass.

Before I knocked, I spit out my gum.

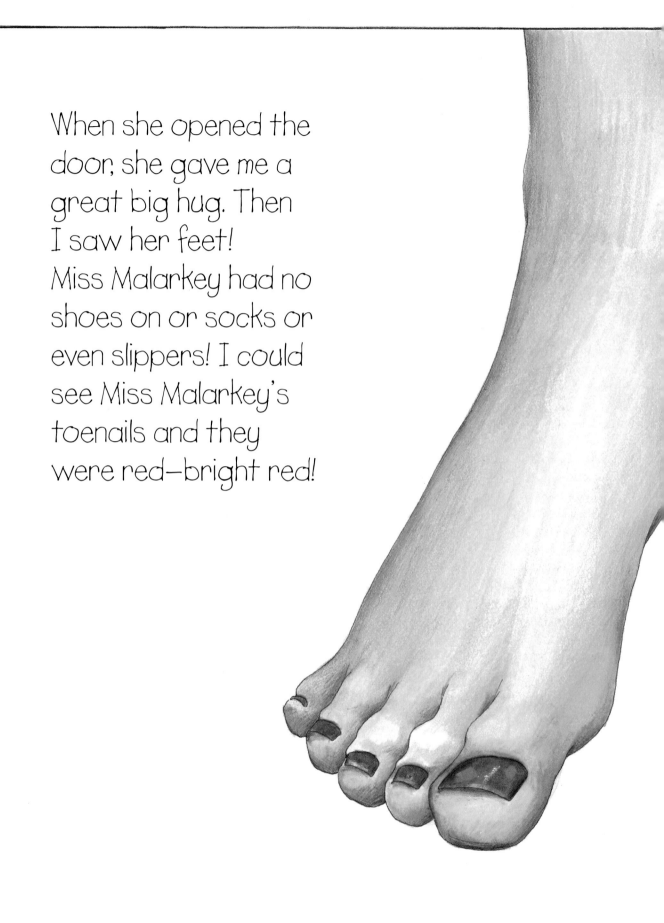

When she opened the door, she gave me a great big hug. Then I saw her feet! Miss Malarkey had no shoes on or socks or even slippers! I could see Miss Malarkey's toenails and they were red—bright red!

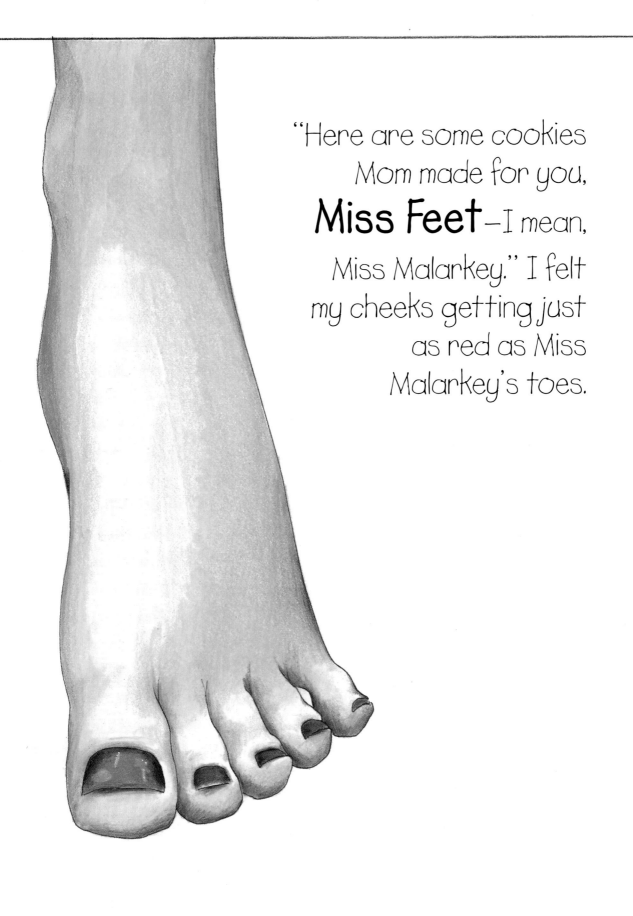

"Here are some cookies
Mom made for you,
Miss Feet–I mean,
Miss Malarkey." I felt
my cheeks getting just
as red as Miss
Malarkey's toes.

That very same day I spotted her
throwing out the garbage.

She never does that at school!

On Saturday I saw some people going
into Miss Malarkey's apartment. She
was having a party.
And it wasn't even someone in the
class's birthday!

I told everyone in *my* class that our teacher doesn't live in *Room 10*. Some of them still didn't believe me. So I showed them.

I like having Miss Malarkey live in the same apartment house as me. But I won't see her so much when I go to second grade.

Next year I'll have
Mrs. Boba. Mrs. Boba
doesn't live in my
building.